Monsters
and Mythical Creatures

Frankenstein

Kris Hirschmann

ReferencePoint
Press®

San Diego, CA

© 2012 ReferencePoint Press, Inc.
Printed in the United States

For more information, contact:
ReferencePoint Press, Inc.
PO Box 27779
San Diego, CA 92198
www.ReferencePointPress.com

LIBRARY OF CONGRESS CATALOGING-IN-PUBLICATION DATA

Hirschmann, Kris, 1967–
  Frankenstein / by Kris Hirschmann.
    p. cm. — (Monsters and mythical creatures series)
  Includes bibliographical references and index.
  ISBN-13: 978-1-60152-180-4 (hardback)
  ISBN-10: 1-60152-180-4 (hardback)
  1. Shelley, Mary Wollstonecraft, 1797–1851. Frankenstein—Juvenile literature. 2. Frankenstein's monster (Fictitious character)—Juvenile literature. 3. Monsters in literature—Juvenile literature. I. Title.
  PR5397.F73H57 2011
  823'.7—dc22
                                                                    2011002145

Contents

Taking His Creator's Name

In the 1818 novel *Frankenstein*, author Mary Shelley sends a collection of reassembled, reanimated body parts on an incredible journey. Brought to life by a scientific genius, Shelley's creature emerges as a virtual animal, then matures into an intellectual being, and ends up a revenge-crazed killer. Readers accompany the monster on this physical and emotional journey—and they are terrified every step of the way. This feeling of brooding horror has kept Shelley's novel alive for nearly 200 years. It has also made Shelley's monster into a household word and cultural icon.

As compelling as he is, though, the monster was not Shelley's focus when she wrote her classic book. He has no name and is not even the novel's main character. The work's title, *Frankenstein*, underscores this fact. Shelley's

Did You Know?

The original *Frankenstein* is subtitled *The Modern Prometheus*, for the Greek myth about a human who is punished for stealing secrets from the gods—much as Victor Frankenstein is punished for his scientific folly.

The monster brought to life in Mary Shelley's book Frankenstein *transforms from animal to intellectual being to revenge-crazed killer, a journey that has been re-created in countless books and movies. Among them is the 1931 Boris Karloff thriller.*

FRANKENSTEIN
A CHILLING THRILLER
Based on a Novel by
MARY WOLLSTONECRAFT SHELLEY
BORIS KARLOFF COLIN CLIVE
MAE CLARK JOHN BOLES
Director JAMES WHALE

novel is actually about Victor Frankenstein, the monster's creator and "father." The true horror of the book, to Shelley, was found in Frankenstein's deeds: his irresponsible scientific exploits and his refusal to accept the consequences of his actions. Frankenstein's monster is portrayed mostly as a result of his creator's folly.

Did You Know?

Since it was first published in 1818, *Frankenstein* has never been out of print.

Today, however, this nameless beast has far surpassed his master in the public eye. Now one of history's most famous monsters, Shelley's creature has appeared in countless books, movies, and TV shows. Musicians sing about him; artists paint him; college professors talk about him. But mostly children—and undoubtedly more than a few adults, too—dream about him. As the embodiment of everything people reject, fear, and wish to destroy, Shelley's creature has become a fixture in humankind's nightmares.

Along the way, he has accomplished a significant feat. He has managed to steal his creator's name and is now known far and wide as "Frankenstein." The creature's author never intended this usage, but perhaps it is fitting. Shelley's monster longed to be accepted and loved by his scientist "father." After nearly 200 years of existence, surely this awful offspring—no matter how unwanted and detested—has earned the right to his family's name.

Chapter 1

A Nightmare Comes True

In 1816 a teenager now known as Mary Shelley set out to write a scary story. The endeavor was just a game, a way to pass the hours during an unusually cold, wet summer. This game, however, was destined to have history-making consequences. Shelley could not have guessed it at the time, but she was about to invent a fiend that would stalk humankind's nightmares for centuries to come. Known today as Frankenstein, Shelley's creation is one of the most terrifying and influential monsters the world has ever known.

A Literary Legacy

Shelley was born Mary Wollstonecraft Godwin on August 30, 1797, in London, England. Her father was a well-known political philosopher named William Godwin. Her mother, Mary Wollstonecraft, was a noted philosopher and feminist. Both parents were writers, and both cared deeply about the pursuit of knowledge. They surrounded themselves with friends who had similar interests. As a result, the Godwin household was always a hotbed of intellectual activity and discussion.

Sadly, Shelley never got to see her mother in this environment. Wollstonecraft died from complications of childbirth just days after her infant daughter was born. But she left an important legacy in the form of her writings. Godwin arranged for his late wife's manuscripts to be published. When the time came, he made sure young Mary read her mother's works. Mary therefore received a thorough feminist education at an early age. She was always taught to think and act independently and to question the nature of things, unlike most other girls of her era.

And Mary's education did not stop there. Godwin introduced his daughter to many famous thinkers of the day, including scientists, politicians, artists, and many others. He also encouraged Mary to read important works covering every imaginable topic. Mary devoured these books with apparent fascination. She also began to write her own material, finding inspiration everywhere she turned.

A Young Woman of "Invincible Perseverance"

Growing up in this manner, Mary blossomed into an unusually mature, curious teenager. Her father described his young daughter as "singularly bold, somewhat imperious, and active of mind. Her desire of knowledge is great, and her perseverance in everything she undertakes almost invincible."[1] Godwin was pleased to see his daughter turning into the strong woman he had hoped she would become.

> ## Did You Know?
>
> When Mary Godwin sat down to create *Frankenstein*, she meant to write just a few pages. Her spouse-to-be, Percy Shelley, encouraged her to develop the idea further.

Mary's independent approach, however, quickly led to unexpected consequences. At age 14, Mary met Percy Bysshe Shelley, a famous poet who spent time with Godwin. Shelley was 21 years old at the time, and he was a married man. But these obstacles did not stop Shelley from admiring and then pursuing young Mary. The pair began a secret love affair that went on for two years without Godwin's knowledge.

In 1814 the affair became public when Shelley and the then 16-year-old Mary fled London to begin a life on the road. The couple traveled from place to place, meeting revolutionary thinkers and writing every day. Shelley strongly encouraged Mary in this activity. Like Godwin, Shelley saw Mary's potential, and he pushed hard to make sure it was realized.

A Tragic Life

Mary Shelley is one of the most tragic figures in literary history. The author's misfortunes began in infancy, when her mother died from complications of childbirth. As an adult, Shelley had four children of her own, three of whom died by the age of three. Her half-sister committed suicide; her 29-year-old husband died in a drowning accident; all of her best friends met untimely fates; and her professional colleagues died off one by one. By the age of 26, Shelley had already written these words in her journal: "The last man! Yes I may well describe that solitary being's feelings, feeling myself as the last relic of a beloved race, my companions extinct before me."

Shelley endured most of her losses after *Frankenstein* was written. Yet Shelley's trials are eerily similar to those suffered by her fictional scientist, Victor Frankenstein, whose loved ones are killed by the monster he creates. Frankenstein ends up alone and shattered, just as Shelley eventually did. This similarity is one of history's saddest—and most ironic—coincidences.

Paula R. Feldman and Diana Scott-Kilvert, eds., *The Journals of Mary Shelley: 1814–1844*, vol. 2. Oxford: Clarendon, 1987, p. 542.

A History-Making Contest

After nearly two years on the road, Mary and Shelley decided to spend the summer in Geneva, Switzerland. They rented a cottage near Lake Geneva. Their friend Lord Byron, a famous poet, and his personal physician, John Polidori, rented another home nearby. The foursome spent most of their time together. As a group they read, wrote, and talked late into the night.

During one of these late-night sessions, the conversation took a spooky turn when the friends started to discuss ghost stories they had read. Convinced that the current group could do a better job, Byron proposed a friendly contest. He suggested that each member of the foursome should write an original horror tale, just for fun. All parties agreed to this proposal and threw themselves into writing their grisly creations.

All, that is, except for Mary. Mary was determined to impress the group, and she wanted to come up with a truly terrifying idea. Such an idea, however, proved elusive. Mary thought and thought, but nothing interested her. Days passed, and still Mary had no clue of what to write.

Inspiration

Inspiration arrived unexpectedly in the middle of a cold, dreary night. Mary was lying half-asleep in bed when a frightful vision started to play out in her head. Many years later, Mary Shelley described her nightmare:

> I saw the pale student of unhallowed [unholy] arts kneeling beside the thing he had put together. I saw the hideous phantasm of a man stretched out, and then, on the working of some powerful engine, show signs of life and stir with an uneasy, half-vital motion. . . . His success would terrify the artist; he would rush away from his odious handiwork, horror-stricken. . . . He would hope that, left to itself, the slight spark of life which he had communicated would fade, that this thing which had received such imperfect animation would subside into dead matter, and he might sleep. . . . He sleeps; but he is awakened; he opens his eyes; behold, the horrid thing stands at his bedside, opening his curtains and looking on him with yellow, watery, but speculative eyes.[2]

At this point, Shelley recalls, she jolted awake, shivering with fear. But her horror was soon replaced by a feeling of elation. "I have

The poet Percy Bysshe Shelley woos a young Mary Godwin. Shelley, whom Mary later married, strongly encouraged her writing.

found it!" she realized. "What terrified me will terrify others; and I need only describe the spectre which had haunted my midnight pillow."[3] The next day, Mary announced that she had thought of a story. Retiring to her chambers, she took up her pen and began to write the work that would be known as *Frankenstein*.

The Basic Story

Today, almost anyone can describe the essential concept of *Frankenstein*. The key scene can be summed up in just a few words: A scientist brings a creature to life.

This moment is certainly central to the novel's story line. But it is just one scene among many. *Frankenstein* covers much more ground than most people realize, featuring a long, twisted plot, a full cast of characters, and a host of philosophical musings. All of the book's people, places, and events contribute to the work's memorable monster. To truly understand the creature, therefore, it is important to understand the full scope of Shelley's literary masterpiece.

The book begins with a series of letters written by Robert Walton, the captain of an Arctic exploration ship. Addressed to Walton's sister in England, the letters explain that the ship has been trapped in an ice field. A castaway has been discovered, half frozen and nearly dead, on a nearby block of ice. The man has been taken onto Walton's ship and is being nursed back to health.

The mysterious castaway turns out to be Victor Frankenstein, a Swiss scientist. Frankenstein recovers quickly under Walton's care and becomes friendly with the lonely captain. Before long, Frankenstein offers to tell Walton a strange tale. At this point Walton's letters end, and Frankenstein's voice takes over the narrative.

Creating a Monster

Frankenstein begins his story with a description of his childhood in Geneva, Switzerland. There he enjoyed the company of his adopted sister Elizabeth Lavenza; his best friend Henry Clerval; and his adoring parents, who nurtured their beloved son both emotionally and intellectually. "No human being could have passed a happier childhood than myself,"[4] Frankenstein wistfully says to Walton.

At the age of 17, Frankenstein leaves his family to attend the University of Ingolstadt in Germany. Frankenstein proves to be a brilliant student and quickly becomes fascinated by the fields of natural philosophy (which today is called natural science) and chemistry. After mastering these topics, he turns his attention to human physiology—and before long, he makes an incredible breakthrough. Frankenstein describes the fateful moment with these words: "A sudden light broke in upon me—a light so brilliant and wondrous, yet so simple. . . . I succeeded in discovering the cause of generation and life; nay, more, I became myself capable of bestowing animation upon lifeless matter."[5]

Frankenstein immediately resolves to put his newfound knowledge to use. He spends months building a humanlike creature out of dead flesh and bones. One dreary autumn night, the task is finally done. Frankenstein animates his creation, expecting it to be beautiful. He is shocked to discover that the creature is hideous instead. Horrified and disgusted, Frankenstein flees to the safety of his bedroom. He soon falls into a fitful sleep but awakens shortly afterward to find the monster standing over his bed.

> ## Did You Know?
> Historians suspect that a substance called laudanum caused Mary Godwin's history-making nightmare. In the early 1800s this mild narcotic was commonly prescribed to relieve coughing, diarrhea, and pain. It was also known to cause hallucinations.

Frankenstein flees once again and spends the rest of the night pacing the streets. When he finally dares to return to his apartment, the monster is gone—but Frankenstein's horror remains. Sick with guilt, Frankenstein falls into a long and feverish illness.

Murder and Mayhem

Frankenstein is nursed back to health by his best friend, Clerval, who has arrived unexpectedly at Ingolstadt. Just as Frankenstein is starting to feel like himself again, terrible news arrives from Switzerland. Fran-

Blood Cousins

The contest that produced *Frankenstein* gave birth to another classic creature as well. As his contribution, Lord Byron spun a story about a blood-sucking vampire aristocrat and his doomed human victims. John Polidori eventually used Byron's yarn as the basis for a tale entitled *The Vampyre*, which was published in 1819. Featuring the terrifying Lord Ruthven, this story is usually cited as the first known work of vampire fiction.

Unlike Mary Shelley's monster, the vampire was not a completely original invention. The bloodthirsty undead had been a staple of European folklore for untold centuries before Polidori put pen to paper. But traditional vampires were usually described as filthy, animallike creatures. *The Vampyre* introduced the entirely novel idea that vampires could appear human. More than that, they could even be attractive and aristocratic. These qualities allowed vampires to walk undetected among people and choose their prey at will.

This notion proved to be frightening, yet endlessly fascinating. It led to a number of other vampire-related works, including one of the most famous horror books of all time: Bram Stoker's *Dracula*. Thanks to this work and thousands of others, the vampire holds a top spot on the list of history's most notorious monsters.

kenstein's five-year-old brother, William, has been murdered. Frankenstein's father begs his oldest son to return home.

Frankenstein immediately heads for Geneva. When he arrives, he pays a nighttime visit to William's grave. There, in a flash of lightning, Frankenstein glimpses the monster he created more than a year earlier. Frankenstein is instantly certain that the creature killed his little brother. Although a dear family friend is eventually tried, convicted, and executed for the crime, Frankenstein remains firm in his belief.

This situation troubles Frankenstein deeply. As the true murderer's creator, Frankenstein feels that he himself is ultimately responsible for his brother's death. Shaken and guilt-ridden, the scientist heads alone into the wilderness. He hopes that distance and fresh air will clear his mind and help him to forget his troubles.

Instead of escaping his problems, however, Frankenstein finds himself in an entirely new nightmare. On a remote mountaintop, the monster suddenly appears and confronts his maker. He demands an audience—and he also delivers an ultimatum. "Do your duty towards me, and I will do mine towards you and the rest of mankind. If you will comply with my conditions, I will leave them and you at peace; but if you refuse, I will glut the maw of death, until it be satiated with the blood of your remaining friends,"[6] the creature threatens.

Feeling that he has little choice, Frankenstein follows his creation to an abandoned hut. There the monster explains how he has spent the time since he last saw his maker. He has learned human speech and habits by secretly observing the residents of a rural hut. He eventually tried to become friends with these people, only to watch his "family" flee in terror. This experience infuriated the monster and blackened his heart—especially against his creator. Angry and lonely, the monster has vowed to make Frankenstein's life miserable.

But the creature offers his creator one way out of this awful situation. The creature wants a bride—a resurrected female, much like himself, to be his companion and ease his loneliness. If Frankenstein will provide this bride, the creature promises to go away. He will never trouble Frankenstein or his loved ones again.

A Grisly Task

Frankenstein is appalled by the monster's offer; however, he is worried about his family's safety and especially about Elizabeth, to whom he is now engaged. He also feels that he owes his creation whatever happiness he can provide. Reluctantly, Frankenstein agrees to create a wife for the monster standing before him.

To perform this dread task, Frankenstein heads for a remote island. There he collects scraps of human flesh and bones, just as he had done in Ingolstadt. The scientist works night and day to fulfill the gruesome promise he has made. Slowly but surely, a female form takes shape in Frankenstein's workshop.

One dark night, when the job is nearly done, Frankenstein starts to question himself. At this moment he looks up to see the monster leering at him through a window, and all doubt is erased. Frankenstein realizes that he cannot release another evil creature upon the world. He tears the still-dead female to pieces and vows that he will never resume his work. The monster, seeing these events, is furious. "You shall repent of the injuries you inflict. . . . I shall be with you on your wedding night,"[7] the creature threatens. But these words do not sway Frankenstein. The scientist throws the bloody bits of his destroyed project into a basket, then heads to sea in a rowboat to dispose of the foul evidence.

When Frankenstein returns to land, he discovers that a new challenge awaits him. The scientist is confronted by a group of villagers, who inform Frankenstein that a murder has occurred. The victim turns out to be Clerval. Frankenstein becomes sick with guilt when he realizes that Clerval, like young William, was killed by the monster—and that more murders will undoubtedly follow. Out of his mind with grief, Frankenstein cannot defend himself when the villagers throw him into jail. He spends months in a filthy cell, raving and close to death, before his father finally arrives to rescue him.

Frankenstein Finale

Sick and weak, Frankenstein returns to his Geneva home. The family decides that after so many tragedies, it would cheer everyone up if Frankenstein and Elizabeth were to marry as quickly as possible. Frankenstein's father proposes a wedding date just 10 days hence.

Frankenstein is very nervous about this development. He loves Elizabeth deeply, but he cannot forget the monster's threats. He fully expects to be murdered on his wedding night. But Frankenstein decides that he cannot put off the dreaded moment forever. He consents to the wedding and throws himself into the preparations. At the same time, he secretly prepares for the fight of his life.

When the big day finally arrives, Elizabeth and Frankenstein are married without incident. Afterward, the newlyweds travel to an inn where they plan to spend their wedding night. Frankenstein, who expects to be attacked at any moment, sends his bride to another room so she will not have to witness anything awful. To his horror, he soon hears Elizabeth screaming. Frankenstein rushes into Elizabeth's room and finds his bride dead—strangled, like so many others, by the creature Frankenstein created.

This event is the final straw for Frankenstein. Realizing that the monster will never cease his ravages, the scientist vows to find and, if possible, destroy his creation. "My rage is unspeakable when I reflect that the murderer, whom I have turned loose upon society, still exists. . . . I devote myself, either in my life or death, to his destruction,"[8] Frankenstein swears.

Frankenstein sets off in pursuit of the monster, who flees northward. The chase continues for months and eventually reaches the Arctic. It is here that Frankenstein gets stuck on an ice floe and is rescued by Walton, bringing the tale back to its starting point.

At this point Walton resumes the story's narrative. Continuing his letters to his sister, Walton explains that Frankenstein weakened and died after telling his tale. Soon afterward, Walton says, he heard a sound in the dead man's chamber and went to investigate. He discovered the monster standing over his creator, weeping. The creature told Walton of his suffering, loneliness, and remorse. He explained that with Frankenstein dead, he is finally free to die, too. He plans to build a bonfire and throw himself into its flames. With these words the creature leaped out of the window and drifted away on the ice, never to be seen again.

Frankenstein Hits the Shelves

It took Mary nearly a year to complete her masterwork. During this period, Shelley's wife died, and he and Mary finally married. Officially known now as Mary Shelley, the young author penned the final words of her novel in May 1817 and submitted the manuscript to several publishers. A small London publishing house called Lackington, Hughes, Harding, Mayor & Jones agreed to accept the project.

The first edition of *Frankenstein; or, the Modern Prometheus* came out on January 1, 1818. The book was published in three volumes, a standard format at the time. It did not carry Mary Shelley's name or, indeed, any name. It was published anonymously, with a preface written on his wife's behalf by Percy Shelley. The novel's first print run was just 500 copies.

Considering its modest beginnings, *Frankenstein* made a significant splash. The work's unusual subject matter generated a great deal of attention and many prominent reviews. These reviews universally assumed that Frankenstein's anonymous author was male—and most of them ripped this unknown author's work to shreds. The worst critiques focused on Shelley's philosophic approach. "Our taste and our judgement alike revolt at this kind of writing . . . it inculcates no lesson of conduct, manners, or morality; it cannot mend, and will not even amuse its readers . . . it fatigues the feelings without interesting the understanding; it gratuitously harasses the sensations,"[9] complained politician and literary critic John Wilson Croker in one scathing review.

Other reviewers took issue not with Shelley's values but with her storytelling skills. "There are gross inconsistencies in the minor details of the story. . . . The whole detail of the development of the creature's mind and faculties is full of [them],"[10] griped one anonymous reviewer. This person felt that Shelley's account of the monster's personal growth was ridiculous and unbelievable in every respect.

The idea for Frankenstein *came about as a result of a friendly competition between the poet Lord Byron (pictured); his personal physician, John Polidori; Percy Shelley; and Mary Godwin. Each member of the group agreed to write an original horror tale.*

Mixed with the negative comments, however, were a few grudging positives. Most of them had to do with Shelley's writing abilities. "The ideas of the author are always clearly as well as forcibly expressed; and his descriptions of landscape have in them the choice requisites of truth, freshness, precision, and beauty,"[11] wrote author Sir Walter Scott in *Blackwood's Edinburgh Magazine*.

Even Croker, who found little to love about Shelley's work, admitted that some of the book's imagery was striking. "*Frankenstein* has passages which appall the mind and make the flesh creep," he said. "The author has powers, both of conception and language."[12]

Lasting Success

From the public's perspective, these positive features evidently outweighed the negatives. *Frankenstein* was an immediate hit despite its lukewarm literary reception. The first edition sold out, leading to a 2-volume reprint in 1823 and a single-volume edition in 1831. The 1831 edition, now bearing Mary Shelley's name, was extensively revised by the author. This version is the text most commonly seen today.

And seen it is. Today Shelley's novel is sold nearly everywhere in the world, in every language. It is required reading in many high schools and colleges, and it appears on virtually every list of must-read classics. With millions upon millions of copies in print, Shelley's opus has proved itself to be a blockbuster of truly monstrous proportions.

Since the mid-1900s, it has been a critical darling as well. Most modern reviewers feel that *Frankenstein*, although flawed, was in many respects a groundbreaking work. The book is often cited as an important example of early romantic and gothic writing, two genres

> ## Did You Know?
>
> The year 1816, when *Frankenstein* was written, is known as "The year without a summer." A severe volcanic eruption caused the wet, cold conditions that spurred Mary Godwin to stay indoors and write her famous novel.

that had a huge impact on literary thought and history. It is remembered as one of the first published works of science fiction. With the benefit of hindsight, today's critics also praise the book for its cutting portrayal of early-1800s European society. Shelley had a keen grasp of many feminist and social issues, and *Frankenstein* displays this knowledge to good effect.

An Immortal Monster

The lasting impact of *Frankenstein*, though, is not due to its stylistic or philosophical content. *Frankenstein* caught, and continues to catch, the public's attention with its grotesque yet all-too-human monster. It seems clear that the dream that spawned Shelley's classic creation is just as frightening today as it was nearly 200 years ago. Or perhaps it is even more frightening, says one reviewer, since nowadays "readers generally [understand] the novel as an evocation of the modern condition: man trapped in a godless world in which science and ethics have gone awry."[13]

This social and technological atmosphere, which Shelley could not have foreseen in 1816, breathes new life into a timeless tale. It keeps *Frankenstein* relevant and grants virtual immortality to its central creature—a hideously stitched-together, reanimated giant bent on murder and revenge. Frankenstein's monster is a kind of worst-case scenario, the most terrifying possible consequence of every unconsidered action. In the modern world, where unconsidered action sometimes seems like the rule rather than the exception, it is no wonder that this idea—and this monster—have found a permanent home in humankind's worst nightmares.

Chapter 2

Anatomy of a Monster

Today, most people—even those who have never read *Frankenstein*—think they know all about Mary Shelley's famous monster. They can describe the creature's looks, his personality, his actions, and the moment he comes to life. They also think they understand *Frankenstein*'s plot. "I just assumed . . . that Dr. Frankenstein went to the cemetery, stole body parts, created a monster, the monster escaped, and the story climaxed as a group of townsmen find the monster and lynch it,"[14] explains one typical nonreader.

Descriptions like this one are colorful, but they are all too often inaccurate. As one critic comments, "The fame of Victor Frankenstein and his creation is based mainly on various adaptations and rewritings of the original 19th-century novel."[15] Most of these adaptations and rewritings have twisted Shelley's original ideas beyond all recognition.

These misconceptions are not hard to correct. Victor Frankenstein's monster is amply described throughout Mary Shelley's best-known novel. So is the scientist himself. A simple read-through provides a very clear picture of Frankenstein's work and his creature's grisly origin, as well as the living monster's body, thoughts, and deeds.

The Spark of Life

The tale of Frankenstein's monster begins with an idea: Would it be possible to animate a nonliving object? Shelley's book explains precisely how

Frankenstein conceived and studied this dread notion. The scientist, during the course of his university studies, became fascinated with the concept of life and longed to know where the "spark" came from. Searching for an answer to this question, Frankenstein developed an obsession with dead bodies. "[I was] forced to spend days and nights in vaults and charnel-houses [places where human remains are stored]. . . . I saw how the fine form of man was degraded and wasted; I beheld the corruption of death,"[16] he explains.

This sickening hobby took a mental toll on Frankenstein, who often felt repulsed by his work. But his efforts were ultimately fruitful. As the result of his gruesome observations, Frankenstein suddenly realizes one day how to create life. Shelley never explains this breakthrough. On the contrary, through Frankenstein's words, she *refuses* to define it. The scientist says several times that he wants to protect others from repeating his actions, as he believes they can only cause destruction and misery. He therefore consistently resists discussing his methods or scientific insights.

The moment of the creature's animation, too, is shrouded in mystery. Shelley does have Frankenstein say that the animation occurred in his workshop, at night, and that it involved scientific instruments of some sort. Other than these scant details, no information is given. From beginning to end, here is Frankenstein's description of the life-giving moment:

> It was on a dreary night of November that I beheld the accomplishment of my toils. With an anxiety that almost amounted to agony, I collected the instruments of life around me, that I might infuse a spark of being into the lifeless thing that lay at my feet. It was already one in the morning; the rain pattered dismally against the panes, and my candle was nearly burnt out, when, by the glimmer of the half-extinguished light, I saw the dull yellow eye of the creature open; it breathed hard, and a convulsive motion agitated its limbs.[17]

Bits and Pieces

Shelley does provide more information when it comes to the creature's physical frame. As the basis for his horrible experiments, Frankenstein assembles a body from bloody, rotting bits and pieces that he gathers over a period of several months. "I collected bones from charnel-houses; and disturbed, with profane fingers, the tremendous secrets of the human frame. . . . The dissecting room and the slaughterhouse furnished many of my materials,"[18] Frankenstein explains.

The author does not elaborate on these actions. However, a couple of assumptions seem reasonable. First, Frankenstein, as a university student, was unlikely to have authorized access to charnel-houses and dissecting rooms. He was probably breaking into these places and stealing the body parts he needed. This activity sheds light on the depth of Frankenstein's obsession.

Also interesting is that Shelley's Frankenstein refers to slaughterhouses as a source for his materials. Only animal remains, not human, would have been available in these facilities. So evidently Frankenstein's creation included chunks of horses, cattle, sheep, and other livestock in addition to human body parts.

Wherever he gets his bits and pieces, Frankenstein takes them back to a secret workshop. There he assembles them, like the dripping pieces of a putrid puzzle. While this process is not described in any detail, Shelley does specify that it is difficult. This difficulty, in fact, leads directly to one of the monster's key physical features: its superhuman size. Frankenstein explains the rationale for the creature's extreme height in this passage:

Although I possessed the capacity of bestowing animation, yet to prepare a frame for the reception of it, with all its intricacies of fibres, muscles, and veins, still remained a work of inconceivable difficulty and labor. . . . As the minuteness of the parts formed a great hinderance to my speed, I resolved . . . to make the being of a gigantic stature; that is to say, about eight feet in height, and proportionably large.[19]

How, exactly, this huge form is held together remains a mystery. Shelley does not describe Frankenstein sewing, or gluing, or stapling anything. The author only tells readers that the work is disgusting: Frankenstein sometimes shudders with horror while carrying out his grisly but life-giving efforts.

A Horrible Creature

Despite his revulsion, the scientist persists in his task. He believes that somehow, the festering body parts he has collected will combine to create a handsome creature. He has given his creation well-proportioned limbs and beautiful features. As a result, he feels sure that the living creature will be pleasing to the eye. The end result of Frankenstein's labors, however, is not what the scientist intends or

Obsessed with death, the scientist in Mary Shelley's story spends untold days and nights studying the human remains stored in charnel-houses. Pictured is a charnel-house in Austria with its collection of human skulls and bones.

expects. Once animated, Frankenstein's creation proves to be hideously ugly. By providing specific information about the creature's looks, Shelley invites readers to share Frankenstein's disgust. One key passage, narrated by Frankenstein, gives the following details: "His yellow skin scarcely covered the work of muscles and arteries beneath; his hair was of a lustrous black, and flowing; his teeth of a pearly whiteness; but these luxuriances only formed a more horrid contrast with his watery eyes, that seemed almost of the same colour as the dun white sockets in which they were set, his shriveled complexion and straight black lips."[20]

Another important paragraph falls near the end of the novel, when Captain Robert Walton discovers the creature standing near Frankenstein's dead body. In a letter to his sister, Walton uses these words to describe the monster he sees before him:

> Over [Frankenstein] hung a form which I cannot find words to describe; gigantic in stature, yet uncouth and distorted in its proportions. As he hung over the coffin his face was concealed by long locks of ragged hair; but one vast hand was extended, in colour and apparent texture like that of a mummy. . . . Never did I behold a vision so horrible as his face, of such loathsome yet appalling hideousness.[21]

These passages and others make it clear that Frankenstein's creation is truly grotesque. They also provide details about size, hair color, teeth, skin tone, and other physical features that help readers to form a mental picture of the monster as Shelley envisioned him.

Not Quite Human

This mental picture is not just about looks. It is also about actions and abilities. Shelley imbues her fictional creature with many nonhuman and, indeed, even superhuman traits.

Many people are surprised to learn that incredible speed is one of these traits. In Shelley's imagination, Frankenstein's monster is not a lumbering, clumsy beast, as he is often portrayed today. He is actually quick and nimble, able to get around in ways that no human

The Real Monster

In an introduction to a recent edition of *Frankenstein*, literary critic Harold Bloom suggests that Victor Frankenstein is more hideous, in many ways, than his famous creation:

> The daemon is superior to his maker both in spirit and in feeling, and so we come both to love him and to fear him. We do not have any particular affect towards the scientist who has both botched his work (the daemon is hideous in appearance) and failed to take responsibility for his creature. . . .
>
> Victor Frankenstein, though he possesses generous impulses, is nothing less than a moral idiot in regard to the "monster" he has created. Even at the end, he cannot understand his own failure of moral imagination, and he dies still misapprehending the nature of his guilt. He is thus at once a great . . . scientist, an astonishing genius at breaking through human limitations, and a pragmatic monster, the true monster of the novel. His trespass is beyond forgiveness, because he is incapable of seeing that he is both a father, and a god, who has failed to love his marred creation.
>
> With these comments, Bloom raises an interesting question: What makes a monster? Is it appearance, or is it action? Critics agree that this question lies at the heart of Mary Shelley's most famous work.

Harold Bloom, introduction to *Mary Shelley's "Frankenstein."* New York: Chelsea House, 1996, p. 6. www.scribd.com.

could ever match. This ability first becomes evident when Frankenstein encounters his creation in a remote mountain region. "I suddenly beheld the figure of [the creature], at some distance, advancing towards me with superhuman speed. He bounded over the crevices in the ice, among which I had walked with caution,"[22] the scientist remembers in one passage.

> ## Did You Know?
>
> Victor Frankenstein never gives his creation a name. He refers to it by many negative terms including "wretch," "creature," "fiend," "daemon," "devil," and "ogre."

This is not the only reference to the monster's agility. This trait is repeatedly mentioned in the narrative. By frequently reminding readers of her creature's speed, Shelley paints a vivid picture of a monster with the terrifying ability to overtake any human at will.

And this is not the creature's only intimidating trait. The monster also seems to be weatherproof, able to endure extremes of temperature that would kill a human being. The monster refers directly to this ability near the end of the novel, when Frankenstein vows to pursue and destroy his creation at all costs. "I seek the everlasting ices of the north, where you will feel the misery of cold and frost to which I am impassive,"[23] the monster sneers.

Along with this comment, the monster's immunity to cold is also presented indirectly throughout *Frankenstein*'s plot. The creature spends a miserable winter in a frigid shed without apparent discomfort, and he later lives among snowy mountain peaks. At one point he also follows Frankenstein to a barren, windy island and lurks outside the scientist's hut for several months, apparently impervious to the elements. These scenarios make it clear that Frankenstein's nemesis has incredible endurance when it comes to bad weather.

In an online review, one first-time *Frankenstein* reader describes how delighted he was to discover this quality and others. "Instead of finding a plodding flat-headed creature with an I.Q. of 3, the monster is actually something worse—he's agile [and] possesses superhuman strength and agility. . . . This Monster is much scarier and worthy of a great story than Hollywood's oaf,"[24] the reader says gleefully. For this person and many others, the chill factor of Shelley's story gets a big boost from the creature's extraordinary abilities.

A Mindless Brute

The monster is inhuman in other ways as well, particularly at the beginning of Shelley's novel. When Frankenstein's creation first comes to life, he cannot think, or talk, or make sense of the world around him. In this regard the monster is much like a newborn baby. Unlike a human infant, however, the creature has full control of his body. He can walk, grasp objects, and perform other physical tasks with ease. Mobile but mindless, the newly animated monster is unpredictable and therefore absolutely terrifying to his creator.

Frankenstein, it turns out, is not the only one who is afraid. His monster also feels confused and fearful. Later in Shelley's novel, the creature himself describes the early part of his existence with these words: "All the events of that period appear confused and indistinct. A strange multiplicity of sensations seized me, and I saw, felt, heard, and smelt, at the same time. . . . I was a poor, helpless, miserable wretch; I knew, and could distinguish, nothing."[25]

This period of sensory overload does not last long. The monster's eyesight, which is blurry at first, starts to improve. The creature begins to distinguish sight from sound and smell from touch. He notices the sun and the moon, a babbling brook, and other objects. He also sees birds and is delighted when he realizes that they are singing. The creature tries, in his brainless fashion, to imitate these songs. But his voice does not yet work properly, and he only manages to scare himself back into silence.

> # Did You Know?
> In many modern portrayals, Frankenstein's monster is afraid of fire. This was not the case with Shelley's original creature, who loves the comfort of a toasty blaze.

These moments and others help readers to understand the monster's early state. They paint a picture of a creature who is physically terrifying but also confused and timid. At this point the monster is a lumbering but ultimately harmless brute.

A Developing Mind

This situation, however, soon changes. Overwhelmed and afraid, the monster takes shelter in an empty shed—and it is here, over the next several months, that a remarkable transformation takes place. By spying on a family that lives in an adjoining cottage, the creature slowly but surely learns human ways. He changes from an animalistic beast into a thinking, feeling, and surprisingly well-spoken being.

The first moment of change occurs when the creature witnesses the family's father comforting his daughter. This tender scene arouses the first positive emotions the creature has ever experienced. "[The father] smiled with such kindness and affection that I felt sensations of a peculiar and overpowering nature: they were a mixture of pain and pleasure, such as I had never before experienced,"[26] the monster recalls later.

Soon after this incident, the creature makes another key discovery. He realizes that the cottagers are using sounds to communicate with each other. By intense observation and study, the creature manages to learn a few words. He also practices speaking these words until he can pronounce them properly. Little by little, the monster's understanding and vocal abilities start to improve.

The real breakthrough occurs when a Turkish refugee and family acquaintance named Safie arrives at the cottage. Safie does not speak the cottagers' language or write its letters. She also does not understand the cottagers' culture or customs. The family spends the next few months educating Safie in these matters, never suspecting that an extra student is peering through a crack in the wall. "My days were spent in close attention, that I might more speedily master the language. . . . I comprehended and could imitate almost every word that was spoken. . . . I also learned the science of letters, as it was taught to the stranger,"[27] the monster explains.

The Golem

Thousands of years before Mary Shelley's *Frankenstein* appeared, animated beings called golems were lurching their way through Jewish folklore. Golems were humanlike creatures molded from inanimate matter, such as clay or mud. A rabbi could bring one of these models to life by writing the Hebrew word for "truth" on its forehead. To deactivate the creature, the rabbi simply erased one letter to change the Hebrew inscription to "death."

The most famous golem story involves a rabbi named Judah Loew ben Bezalel, also known as the Maharal. In the sixteenth century, the Maharal is said to have created a golem to defend the Jews of Prague. The golem was helpful at first. Over time, however, the creature became increasingly strong, angry, and violent. The rabbi was eventually forced to deactivate the golem and hide his remains in a synagogue attic.

The building where these events supposedly occurred still stands today. Known as the Old-New Synagogue, this structure is the oldest active synagogue in Europe. The building does have an attic, which was sealed from all access for hundreds of years. When the attic was finally explored, no golem was found. Believers must decide for themselves whether the creature was ever there in the first place.

In the introduction to a 1996 edition of *Frankenstein*, literary critic Harold Bloom calls special attention to this scene. "One way to measure the vast distance between Mary Shelley's daemon and the movies' monster is to try to imagine any one of the film monsters educating himself by reading [books]. Mary Shelley's formidable daemon does exactly that, and receives a superb education in consequence,"[28] he says. The creature may have monstrous qualities, but he is also sensitive and literate—qualities that have been largely lost in modern versions of Shelley's tale.

Longing for Love

The creature uses his newfound intellectual skills mostly to muse upon the human condition, which he finds fascinating and altogether enchanting. He decides that people are wonderful—and he starts to crave their companionship above all other things.

At the same time, the creature's budding self-awareness allows him to see himself clearly for the first time. The monster realizes that he is anything but human, and he fears he will never find the love and acceptance for which he yearns. "Increase of knowledge only discovered to me more clearly what a wretched outcast I was. I cherished hope, it is true; but it vanished when I beheld my person reflected in water, or my shadow in the moonshine,"[29] he explains miserably.

Still, the creature is hopeful. Despite his terrifying looks and shape, he knows that he has a kind heart. He feels sure that he will find acceptance and even love, if only he can convince people to overlook his awful appearance. "I imagined that they would be disgusted, until, by my gentle demeanour and conciliating words, I should first win their favour, and afterwards their love,"[30] he says.

Searching for Acceptance

This certainty drives the creature's actions for a short time. Determined to find his place among humans, the monster first introduces himself to his unsuspecting host family. This effort ends in disaster when the terrified family drives the creature from their cottage, then flees the region to escape their horrible visitor. At first the monster is devastated by this turn of events, but his sadness soon turns to fury. "For the first time the feelings of revenge and hatred filled my bosom. . . . When I reflected that they had spurned and deserted me, anger returned, a rage of anger,"[31] says the creature. Overwhelmed by these feelings, the monster commits his first evil act: He sets the family's cottage on fire and watches as it burns to the ground.

This fit of rage, however, soon passes. The creature realizes that he still craves human companionship and love. He decides to seek Frankenstein, his creator, whom he considers his father. The monster sets off on the long journey to Switzerland with a heart full of love and hope. He is willing to overcome any hardship to find the acceptance he seeks.

But along the way, something happens that forever changes the creature's outlook. Traveling through the woods one day, the monster sees a young girl fall into a raging river. He rescues the child at considerable risk to himself and sets her gently on the riverbank. He is trying to resuscitate the child when a townsman appears and shoots the creature in the shoulder. The man then grabs the child and runs away.

This incident proves to be the last straw. Wounded and miserable, the creature abandons all feelings of love and kindness toward human beings. These feelings are replaced by a burning, unquenchable anger. "Inflamed by pain, I vowed eternal hatred and vengeance to all mankind. . . . My daily vows rose for revenge—a deep and deadly revenge, such as would alone compensate for the outrages and anguish I had endured,"[32] the creature swears.

The slaughtered carcasses of pigs (pictured), horses, sheep, and other livestock provided body parts for Victor Frankenstein's monster. The scientist also combed charnel-houses and dissecting rooms in search of human remains for his creation.

Driven by Revenge

Before long, these feelings find a focus. The monster starts to think more and more often about Frankenstein. He develops a deep resentment toward his creator, who never provided the love and guidance the monster feels he is owed. "Unfeeling, heartless creator! you had endowed me with perceptions and passions, and then cast me abroad an object for the scorn and horror of mankind," he groans. "The mildness of my nature had fled, and all within me was turned to gall and bitterness. The nearer I approached to your habitation, the more deeply did I feel the spirit of revenge enkindled in my heart."[33]

From this point onward, rage and bitterness are the creature's defining traits. The monster devotes all of his energy to making Frankenstein's life miserable. He is willing to do anything to accomplish this goal, even to commit murder. The creature discovers, in fact, that he actually enjoys the act of killing, which makes him feel powerful for the first time in his life. People have always made the monster feel bad; now he knows how to make them feel bad in return. It is a transforming moment for the creature, who resolves never to be helpless again.

> ## Did You Know?
>
> Frankenstein's monster finds and reads three classic books at one point in Mary Shelley's novel. These books are John Milton's *Paradise Lost*, Johann Wolfgang von Goethe's *The Sorrow of Werter*, and Plutarch's *Lives*.

The creature is now a killer at heart. But he is still a rational being, and he has the ability to control his murderous urges. At one point he even promises to change his behavior permanently if Frankenstein will build him a wife. When Frankenstein refuses to comply, however, the monster abandons all restraint. He curses his creator once and for all with these awful words:

"I will revenge my injuries: if I cannot inspire love, I will cause fear; and chiefly towards you my arch-enemy, because my creator, do I swear inextinguishable hatred. Have a care: I will work at your destruction, nor finish until I desolate your heart, so that you shall curse the hour of your birth."[34]

At this point in the novel, the monster has completed his transformation. Once gentle, loving, and docile, Frankenstein's creation is now angry and vicious. The changes that occur in the monster have been portrayed much differently in most movies. In films, explains one critic, the monster's evil nature is generally caused by "the brain used, which almost invariably is a criminal brain, or is damaged before implantation. In the book, the creature is really a child that's horribly neglected, but with the strength and intelligence to strike back."[35] Shelley imagined a creature who is evil because of circumstances, not because he is made that way.

And he is not all evil, either. He is also capable, educated, and well-spoken—but these abilities, rather than making the creature seem more human, simply underscore his monstrosity. A slave to his baser emotions and impulses, the creature uses his human faculties to plan and execute a host of terrifyingly inhuman acts.

The Only Escape

The monster is not blind to the irony of this situation. On the contrary, he is keenly aware of the depths to which he has sunk. This fact becomes clear near the end of Shelley's novel, when Walton encounters Frankenstein's creation on his ship. During the conversation that follows, the monster muses with remarkable insight and eloquence on his fall from grace:

> Once I falsely hoped to meet with beings who, pardoning my outward form, would love me for the excellent qualities which I was capable of unfolding. I was nourished with high thoughts of honour and devotion. But now crime has degraded me beneath the meanest animal. No guilt, no mischief, no malignity, no misery, can be found comparable to mine. When I run over the frightful catalogue of my sins, I cannot believe that I am the same creature whose thoughts were once filled with sublime and transcendent visions of the beauty and the majesty of goodness. But it is even so; the fallen angel becomes a malignant devil.[36]

It turns out that this "devil," however, retains a speck of humanity. When Frankenstein dies, his creation does not turn unrestrainedly to evil. Instead, he loses his motivation and his will to live. The only emotion the creature can muster is self-loathing—and his only recourse is oblivion. "Some years ago . . . I should have wept to die; now it is my only consolation,"[37] the beast says to Walton before fleeing into the wilderness and, presumably, to his death.

This ending is undeniably tragic, but it is somehow hopeful as well. By wishing to die, the monster proves that evil is not insurmountable. No one, Shelley seems to be saying—not even an actual monster—can live with the consequences of monstrous behavior. This warning, which is just as relevant to modern readers as it was to Shelley's nineteenth-century audience, is undoubtedly part of *Frankenstein*'s enduring impact and popularity.

Chapter 3

Retelling the Tale on Stage and Screen

In 1818 Mary Shelley's chilling tale of science gone amok was a huge hit with the reading public. Not surprisingly, therefore, *Frankenstein* soon made the leap into other entertainment genres. The story first departed from the printed page in 1823, when Victor Frankenstein and his infamous creation made their stage debut. Since then hundreds of other theater, movie, and TV productions have followed.

Frankenstein-themed retellings and adaptations have taken many different approaches. Some have been faithful or near faithful renditions of Shelley's story. Others have been out-and-out fabrications, only thinly based on the author's original work. Whatever approach they take, these productions have kept Mary Shelley's legacy alive while shaping—or, some would say, distorting—the popular image of Frankenstein's monster.

The Story Hits the Stage

The reshaping process began in 1823 with a London-based stage production entitled *Presumption; or, the Fate of Frankenstein*. Directed by Richard Brinsley Peake, the show ran for 37 performances before closing its curtains. Mary

Shelley herself attended one of these performances. The author enjoyed the show but felt that it departed too far from the original plot. "The story was not well managed,"[38] she later complained to a friend.

This reaction is understandable. Peake's production did take a great many liberties with Shelley's work. Key characters were changed, eliminated, or added, and some story elements were altered beyond all recognition. Most significant, though, were the changes made to the monster himself. In *Presumption*, the creature is a speechless brute with an infantile mind. He certainly cannot reason or plot revenge, as he does in Shelley's novel. He can only feel rage and commit acts of random violence against his creator and others. With these changes, *Presumption* presented an entirely new twist on Frankenstein's monster.

In 1826 a play entitled *Frankenstein; or, The Man and the Monster* added another element to the mix. It took the audience into Frankenstein's laboratory to witness, for the first time ever, the moment when the scientist animates his creation. The playwright, Henry M. Milner, included explicit instructions for this scene in his script: "Laboratory with bottles and chemical apparatus. First sight of the monster an indistinct form with a black cloth ... music .... A colossal human figure of a cadaverous livid complexion, it slowly begins to rise, gradually attaining an erect posture. When it has attained a perpendicular position, and glares its eyes upon him, he starts back with horror."[39]

Something Entirely New

In modern terms, this vision is not particularly gruesome or inventive. It probably would not shock or even surprise today's audiences, who have seen countless *Frankenstein*-inspired animation scenes. To nineteenth-century viewers, however, Milner's monstrous creation scenario was something entirely new, and it was a big hit. People

A huge, corpselike human figure lies inert on a table in Victor Frankenstein's lab in the moments before the scientist brings his creation to life. This scene from the 1944 movie House of Frankenstein *harks back to an 1826 play based on Shelley's story.*

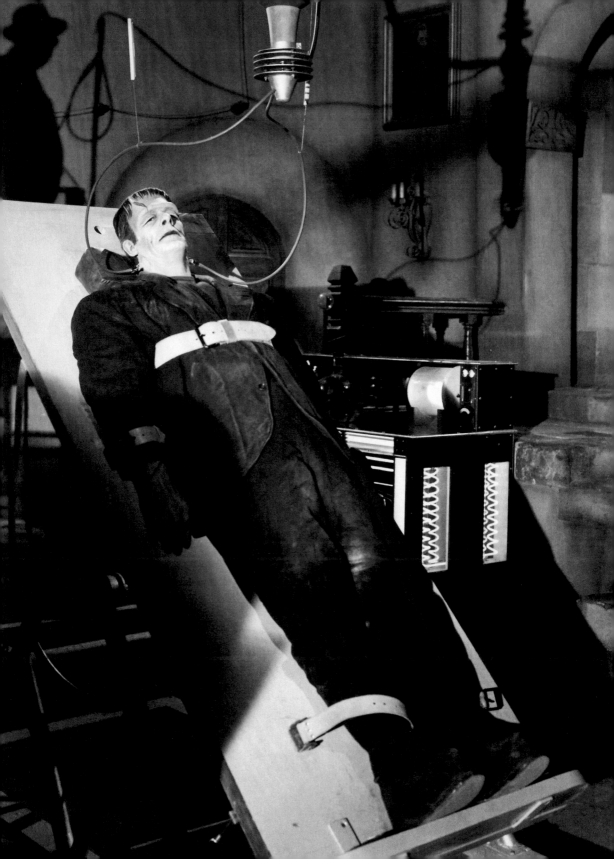

were fascinated by Frankenstein's loathsome laboratory, and they wanted to see more—the grislier, the better.

They have gotten their wish. Shelley's classic horror tale has continued to inspire playwrights all the way into the present age. Nearly 100 stage versions of *Frankenstein* now exist. These versions, although very different from each other, all have something in common: They let people actually see the horrible being that plagues Frankenstein. By doing so, they increase people's understanding and appreciation of Shelley's novel. "In bearing witness to the hideous visage of the monster, the audience immediately shares Frankenstein's repulsion and understands his desire to escape,"[40] explains one writer.

The Silent Era

This experience may have started with stage productions, but it did not end there. Audiences got a whole new way to share Frankenstein's experiences in 1910, when the first *Frankenstein*-themed film was released. Entitled simply *Frankenstein*, the 12-minute feature is a silent movie set to piano music. Directed by J. Searle Dawley and produced by the Edison Film Company, the film tells a highly abbreviated version of Shelley's tale.

The first *Frankenstein* film is notable for several reasons. First and foremost is its portrayal of the monster itself. The creature in this movie is an explosively hairy beast with enormous, clown-like feet and elongated fingers. It is generally human in size and shape, but it seems more like an enraged gorilla than a person. Creepy yet somehow comical as well, the monster does not project any sense of profound menace.

The same cannot be said of the movie's creation scene, which is surprisingly grisly considering its early origins. The life-giving mo-

> # Did You Know?
>
> At the end of the 1823 play *Presumption,* Victor Frankenstein and his creation perish together in an avalanche. Frankenstein causes the avalanche by shooting a gun at his monster.

The Story Starts

Three films tell the story of *Frankenstein*'s origin, using Mary Shelley (then Mary Godwin) and her compatriots as characters. The first of these films, *Gothic*, came out in 1986. Starring Gabriel Byrne, Julian Sands, and Natasha Richardson, this highly fictionalized account depicts one horrible night during which the characters suffer a series of twisted nightmares. The novel *Frankenstein* arises from this awful evening.

The 1988 film *Haunted Summer* tackles the same topic in a much different way. Starring Alice Krige as *Frankenstein*'s eventual author, this movie explores the interactions between Mary Godwin, Percy Shelley, Lord Byron, and John Polidori during the fateful summer of 1816. Together the four writers discuss life and philosophy, play manipulative mind games, and experience various romantic liaisons. These activities foster an atmosphere of simmering creativity that ends in an outpouring of literary horror.

A film entitled *Rowing with the Wind* also came out in 1988. Like *Haunted Summer*, this movie focuses mostly on Mary Godwin and her human companions rather than on Frankenstein or his famous monster. Starring the powerhouse duo of Hugh Grant and Elizabeth Hurley, the film is sleek, stylish, and quite accurate in its portrayal of Mary Shelley's tragic life.

ment involves a bubbling cauldron into which Frankenstein tosses handfuls of chemicals, like a demented chef seasoning a reeking stew. The creature's form erupts from this concoction one bloody bit at a time, writhing and wriggling in apparent agony as it grows. The process lasts for about two minutes, providing ample opportunity for viewers—even modern ones—to squirm with disgust. Imaginative, original, and altogether awful, this scene set a chilling standard for all *Frankenstein*-themed films to follow.

And follow they soon did. Another silent movie entitled *Life Without Soul* appeared in 1915. Directed by Joseph W. Smiley, this film was shot in various locations around the United States. It features a scientist called Dr. William Frawley (the name Frankenstein is not used) who creates a soulless monster that is clearly based on Shelley's creation. The monster kills Frawley's sister, then flees across Europe with Frawley in hot pursuit. Frawley eventually corners and fatally shoots his creation—but the effort proves to be the doctor's undoing. Mortally tired from his long chase, Frawley sickens and soon dies of exhaustion.

Less is known about the plot of *Il Mostro di Frankenstein* ("The Monster of Frankenstein"), a 1920 Italian film produced by Luciano Albertini and directed by Eugenio Testa. This film is now considered lost, with no known copies in existence today. The story line reputedly included a confrontation between Frankenstein and his monster that was lifted straight from Shelley's novel. But not much else is known about this movie, which marked the end of *Frankenstein*'s silent-film run.

> **Did You Know?**
>
> A Broadway adaptation of *Frankenstein* played for just one performance on January 4, 1981. Featuring several big-name stars, this play was the most expensive flop ever produced to that date.

Milestone Moment

The end of one film era marked the beginning of another. By the late 1920s, film technology had improved to the point that talking motion pictures were possible. This development paved the way for *Frankenstein*'s film career to take off in a truly monstrous fashion.

The first and arguably the best entry in this foul filmography occurred in 1931 with the release of Universal Pictures' *Frankenstein*. Directed by James Whale and starring Boris Karloff as the monster, this movie is far from a faithful adaptation of Shelley's work. It changes names, events, and key aspects of the novel on which it is based. But despite these liberties, the 1931 *Frankenstein* turned out to be astonishingly effective. In terms of both plot and imagery, it came to define Shelley's creature in the public eye.

The credit for this impact goes largely to the film's director along with Jack Pierce, Universal's then chief makeup artist. The two men discussed their visions of Shelley's monster and came up with a being that one critic terms "the most influential horror image of all times."[41] The monster in question was enormous but subtly misshapen, with corpselike skin and scraggly black hair. Heavy brows shaded the creature's eyes, which were half-hidden under permanently droopy lids. Electrical-looking metal bolts protruded from the creature's neck, and rows of sloppy stitches criss-crossed its absurdly large, squared-off head. Huge, ungainly, and ugly, Karloff's character is the vision most people see today when they hear the name "Frankenstein."

Along with this visually striking antihero came another innovation: a whole new creation scenario. In Whale's film, Frankenstein's nonliving assemblage of flesh and bones lies amidst electrical devices and bubbling test tubes on a platform. The platform rises to the top of the lab during a thunderstorm, allowing the creature it bears to be animated by a stroke of lightning. Frankenstein's famously hysterical cry, "It's alive! Alive!,"[42] was uttered for the first time in this groundbreaking scene.

This moment and others in Whale's production struck an immediate chord with the viewing public. *Frankenstein* was a huge hit at the box office, earning dozens of times what it had cost to make. The movie was also a critical darling, earning a nod from the *New York Times* as one of the best films of the year. In both sales and reception, it was Universal Pictures' biggest success up to that point.

Did You Know?

During the filming of 1931's *Frankenstein*, Boris Karloff spent over three hours each morning in the makeup chair to achieve his monstrously famous look.

Building on Success

Not surprisingly, Universal then sought to repeat this success with a sequel. *Bride of Frankenstein*, which reunited the team of James Whale, Jack Pierce, and Boris Karloff, hit theater screens in 1935. The plot of this film concerns the evil Dr. Pretorius, who forces Frankenstein to create a female mate for his monster. Frankenstein reluctantly complies—but the result is not what anyone expects. Appalled and terrified by her proposed mate, the reanimated woman rejects Frankenstein's original creature. This disappointment is the final straw for the monster, who destroys Pretorius, the bride, and finally himself in a fit of rage. "You live! We belong dead!"[43] the beast (who can now mumble a few words) says bitterly to Frankenstein in his dying moments.

In financial terms, *Bride of Frankenstein* was something of a disappointment for Universal Pictures. It earned only a fraction of *Frankenstein*'s box office returns. As part of the Frankenstein catalog, however, this film stands as a milestone moment. It introduced several important changes to the monster's image, giving the creature the ability to speak, to laugh, to socialize with humans, and even to feel love. These changes brought a little bit of Shelley's original intent into the public eye. "While in *Frankenstein* [the Monster] was a murderous vengeful creature, the sequel presents a Monster the audience can sympathise with, thus bringing him much closer to Mary Shelley's original concept,"[44] explains one critic.

This true-to-life approach, however, was completely abandoned in Universal's third Frankenstein picture. With new director Rowland V. Lee at the helm, the 1939 film *Son of Frankenstein* bore virtually no relationship, plotwise, to Shelley's work. The creature took

> # Did You Know?
>
> Actor Béla Lugosi, who was already famous for playing Dracula on-screen, was the producers' first choice to be the monster in the 1931 version of *Frankenstein*. Lugosi turned down the role because it had no dialogue.

"On Broadway Bride of the busin... at ROXY is grabbing the business far outdistancing everything else... there is no comparison"...Variety

Carl Laemmle presents
KARLOFF
in a Universal picture
Bride of **FRANKENSTEIN**
WITH
COLIN CLIVE · VALERIE HOBSON
ELSA LANCHESTER · UNA O'CONNOR
O.P. HEGGIE   ERNEST THESIGER
Directed by James Whale
Produced by Carl Laemmle, Jr.

In the 1935 film Bride of Frankenstein *the scientist is forced to create a mate for his monster. Though not a big moneymaker, the film introduced new characteristics to the monster, including the ability to speak, to laugh, and even to feel love.*

a major step backward as well, becoming once again a mute, brutal, animalistic beast. The film was popular with audiences, though, and so the changes stuck. From this point onward, Frankenstein's creature was most often portrayed as a true monster.

Another change stuck as well. In *Son of Frankenstein*, the life-giving scientist (who, as the title suggests, is Victor Frankenstein's son) complains frequently that people have started calling his father's creation by the family name: Frankenstein. The scientist might have disliked this development, but audiences loved it. They finally

Imagining a Monster

The striking makeup worn by Boris Karloff in Universal Pictures' 1931 masterpiece, *Frankenstein*, has come to define Victor Frankenstein's monstrous creation in the public mind. A 1939 interview reveals that Jack Pierce, the makeup artist responsible for Karloff's look, did not depend on imagination alone when he dreamed up this image. Pierce describes his creative process in this passage:

> I spent three months of research in anatomy, surgery, medicine, criminal history, criminology, ancient and modern burial customs, and electrodynamics. My anatomical studies taught me that there are six ways a surgeon can cut the skull in order to take out or put in a brain. I figured that Frankenstein, who was a scientist but no practising surgeon, would take the simplest surgical way. He would cut the top of the skull off straight across like a potlid, hinge it, pop the brain in, and then clamp it on tight. That is the reason I decided to make the Monster's head square and flat like a shoe box and dig that big scar across his forehead with the metal clamps holding it together.

Pierce's research allowed him to create a look that was not only creepy but scientifically plausible as well. This touch of reality is undoubtedly part of the reason Pierce's creation touched such a chord—and earned such lasting fame.

Quoted in Alberto Manguel, *BFI Film Classics: "Bride of Frankenstein."* London: British Film Institute, 1997, pp. 20–21.

had a name for their favorite movie monster. Frankenstein the beast became—and Frankenstein he stayed. All future films would refer to the creature in this manner.

Some of these films were additional Universal Pictures offerings. Following *Son of Frankenstein* the studio rapidly released five more Frankenstein-themed movies, including cinematic gems such as *The Ghost of Frankenstein* (1942), *Frankenstein Meets the Wolf Man* (1943), and *House of Frankenstein* (1944). Each of these pictures was more outlandish than the last, and each one took Shelley's monster a bit further from his literary origins. Now a public institution, the creature was developing an image that far exceeded his author's wildest expectations.

Hammering It Home

This development process took a short break after 1948, when Universal Pictures released its final Frankenstein offering. The Frankenstein franchise, however, was much too good to stay dead forever. Shelley's monster was soon reanimated by a British company called Hammer Films, which in 1957 released a movie called *The Curse of Frankenstein*. Directed by Terence Fisher and featuring actor Christopher Lee as Frankenstein (as the creature was now known), this film heralded the big-screen comeback of history's favorite movie monster.

Hammer Films faced a significant challenge in mounting this comeback. Universal Pictures had threatened to sue Hammer if the studio copied Universal's signature Frankenstein makeup. So to avoid a lawsuit, Hammer had to come up with an entirely new look for Shelley's monster. The result of these efforts was a monster that looked nothing like Universal's iconic creature.

But the fiend was hideously memorable nonetheless. Hammer's Frankenstein had scarred, blistered skin and one dead, protruding eyeball. A row of metal staples ran across his forehead, visually implying the grim surgery that had installed Frankenstein's brain. The monster had rotten, uneven teeth and a badly damaged neck that constantly shed bits of bloody, decaying flesh. He was utterly revolting—and audiences found him utterly captivating as well. People came in droves to see *The Curse of Frankenstein*, making the film a huge box office hit.

Considering this success, more Hammer productions would inevitably follow. The company began churning out Frankenstein films, starting with a 1958 sequel entitled *The Revenge of Frankenstein*. Four more movies, including *The Evil of Frankenstein* (1964), *Frankenstein Created Woman* (1967), *Frankenstein Must Be Destroyed* (1969), and *The Horror of Frankenstein* (1970), hit the big screen in rapid succession.

Hammer's run finally ended in 1974 with *Frankenstein and the Monster from Hell*. Although critics agreed that this movie was interesting and well made, the public had apparently lost interest in Hammer's efforts. The film bombed at the box office, putting an end—for the moment—to Frankenstein's big-screen career.

Frankenstein on the Small Screen

Yet still the monster refused to die. As the Hammer era wound down, retellings of Shelley's tale were finding their way onto small screens around the world.

One early production of note appeared as part of the 1968 British series *Mystery and Imagination*. This series featured dramatizations of classic horror stories—and Shelley's *Frankenstein*, of course, fit perfectly into this format. The tale was presented very much in its original spirit, with characters and plotlines intact. The filming style, which one analyst describes as "visually innovative . . . 'arty' whilst at the same time commercial and popular,"[45] made this retelling a worthy addition to the Frankenstein canon.

Another faithful rendition was producer Dan Curtis's *Frankenstein*, a made-for-TV movie that debuted on ABC's *Wide World of Mystery* in 1973. Viewers enjoyed actor Bo Svenson's portrayal of Frankenstein's monster, who appeared dangerous but also confused and sensitive. "Such traits have always been the essence of Shelley's iconic figure; Svenson expertly understands and embodies [this]," says one reviewer, who also dubs the adaptation "a must to view and own."[46]

Notable Interpretations of a Classic Story

Many people feel the same way about another 1973 production entitled *Frankenstein: The True Story*. Although not a direct adaptation of Shelley's novel, this TV movie did incorporate many of its key themes. It was notable for its unusual presentation of Frankenstein's monster, who initially appears as a jaw-droppingly attractive man. Frankenstein is delighted with his work—until, that is, the creature's body starts to disintegrate. Treated with increasing scorn and disgust, the decaying monster becomes bitter. He turns to evil and wreaks havoc on everyone and everything in his path.

And the death and destruction did not stop there. Several later TV versions of *Frankenstein* kept Shelley's story alive to more or less faithful degrees. A British adaptation got good reviews in 1984. A 1992 version made waves on America's TNT cable network. And the Hallmark Channel's 2004 *Frankenstein*, a four-hour extravaganza that boasted Oscar-winning actor William Hurt among its cast, is considered the must-see version by many Frankenstein fanatics. "Mary Shelley describes a being with long, black hair, yellow complexion, and sunken eyes. This is what we get!! Perfect!! . . . Finally, a true to life interpretation of a classic that in all rights should be considered a classic in itself,"[47] raves one happy viewer.

> ## Did You Know?
>
> The film *Son of Frankenstein* introduced a deformed, evil assistant named Ygor. Today, the Ygor or Igor character is an icon in Frankenstein-themed works.

Taking Liberties

As this person points out, faithful-to-the-letter adaptations can be very satisfying. But millions upon millions of Frankenstein fans have discovered over the decades that a less-than-faithful approach has its appeal, too. Some very popular (and some not-so-popular) Frankenstein-related offerings have taken enormous liberties with Shelley's story.

A 1974 film entitled *Young Frankenstein* is a standout entry in this category. Directed by Mel Brooks and starring comedian Gene Wilder along with many other hilarious actors, this movie spoofs Universal's original *Frankenstein* and *Bride of Frankenstein*. The gags never let up in this side-splitting production, which ranks number 13 on the American Film Institute's list of 100 Funniest Films. Among many other classic moments, the movie features actor Peter Boyle as Frankenstein's monster clumsily tap-dancing to the song "Puttin' On the Ritz." The monster ends up stage-diving the horrified audience after being booed and pelted with rotten cabbages that theatergoers have inexplicably stashed within their evening gowns and tuxedo jackets.

Another classically funny spoof is the 1948 film *Abbott and Costello Meet Frankenstein*. The final entry in Universal Pictures' Frankenstein franchise, this movie introduces the famous comedy duo of Bud Abbott and Lou Costello to Frankenstein's monster. The result is a lot of laughs—and a few good scares as well. Now considered a classic, this film too appears on the American Film Institute's list, coming in as the fifty-sixth funniest film ever made.

> **Did You Know?**
>
> *The Curse of Frankenstein* was the first Frankenstein-themed movie to be filmed in color.

Funny for those who like their chills on the campy side is *The Rocky Horror Picture Show*. In this 1975 cult classic, an innocent young couple enters the castle of the evil, cross-dressing, and possibly alien Dr. Frank-N-Furter. They are present when Frank-N-Furter animates his "creature," which in this case is a young blond beefcake with six-pack abs and shimmering gold short-shorts. Misunderstandings, mayhem, and musical numbers galore ensue, creating a production that one critic terms "the shining textbook example of a film so bad it's good."[48]

Many other Frankenstein-themed films have tried to achieve this standard. Virtually all of them, unfortunately, have failed miserably. Shelley's story has inspired a host of imaginative but awful clunkers, including *I Was a Teenage Frankenstein* (1957), *Frankenstein Meets the*

Space Monster (1965), the blaxploitation film *Blackenstein* (1973), and even the Western-flavored *Jesse James Meets Frankenstein's Daughter* (1966). Featuring no-name casts and restrictive budgets, movies like these add little of substance to the Frankenstein mystique.

Big Budgets, Big Names

Other productions, however, have had a much larger impact. Since the mid-1980s, several major Frankenstein-related movies have made their way onto theater screens. Featuring big stars and big budgets, these films have exposed a whole new generation of movie-goers to Shelley's classic tale.

A 1985 film called *The Bride* started this trend. This movie, which is based on the 1935 *Bride of Frankenstein*, stars pop star Sting as Victor Frankenstein and actress Jennifer Beals as the reanimated bride. "Eva," as the bride is called, is a lovely and human-seeming woman.

Her intended mate, however, is anything but human. The attempt to unite these equal-but-opposite beings forms the heart of this movie, which enjoys a devoted following among Frankenstein fans.

The film *Van Helsing*, which was released in 2004, has earned a huge fan base as well. Starring Hugh Jackman and Kate Beckinsale, this special-effects extravaganza bears no resemblance to *Frankenstein* the novel, and it mostly concerns vampires. However, a version of Frankenstein's monster does feature prominently in the film's far-fetched plot. Literate and sensitive, this creature seems very similar—in personality, at least—to Shelley's original invention.

For the ultimate Shelley experience, though, true fans turn to a film called *Mary Shelley's Frankenstein*. This 1994 production was directed by renowned Irish actor Kenneth Branagh, who also portrays Frankenstein on-screen. Equally renowned actor Robert De Niro plays the role of the creature. The animation scene in this film is harrowing, with the monster emerging clumsily from a vat of amniotic fluid. Frankenstein struggles briefly with his creation before fleeing, leaving the gooey monster lying helpless on the floor. "The image I had in mind for the birth sequence is of a child being born to parents who then walk out of the delivery room and leave this bloodstained, fluid covered thing to just crawl around on its own,"[49] Branagh explained in a later interview.

Modern Retellings Capture Audiences

Interestingly, this shocking and gruesome image occurs in a so-called "faithful" adaptation of Shelley's work. Shelley never described any such occurrence, and indeed, the attempt would have been considered inappropriate in Shelley's time. Yet Branagh's concept perfectly captures the heart-wrenching abandonment of Shelley's creature—and modern audiences, who are much more jaded than those of the 1800s, are more than willing to watch. This scene proves that modern retellings can capture and sometimes even enhance classic stories, even one as iconic as *Frankenstein*.

Chapter 4

Frankenstein in Popular Culture

On the final pages of *Frankenstein*, the monster announces his plan to commit suicide. "I shall collect my funeral pile and consume to ashes this miserable frame. . . . I shall die,"[50] he tells Captain Robert Walton. The creature then disappears into the Arctic night where, presumably, he executes his fiery sentence.

With this passage, Mary Shelley ruthlessly kills off her famous fiend. Like all great horror icons, however, Frankenstein's monster has stubbornly refused to die. Shelley's creation—or a semblance of it, at least—is very much alive and well today in countless formats. From novels to comics, cartoons to conversations, Frankenstein's monster stomps his way through practically every aspect of modern popular culture.

TV Fodder

The most visible part of this journey has occurred on the television screen. Creatures clearly inspired by Shelley's monster pop up regularly in sitcoms, dramas, action shows, and every other type of TV offering. The stories being told in these episodes have little or nothing to do with Shelley's original work. They put their own modern spins on Shelley's most famous creation.

A comedy called *The Munsters* is probably the best-known of these offerings. This black-and-white show, which originally aired from 1964 to 1966, showcases the adventures of a not-too-scary monster family. The father and head of the clan, Herman Munster, looks a great deal like the 1931 movie version of Frankenstein's monster. His behavior, however, is very different. Played by actor Fred Gwynne, Herman Munster is a lovable, gentle, well-spoken oaf with a tendency to throw childish temper tantrums. He stomps his huge feet during these moments, bringing ceiling plaster raining down on his family's heads.

The Addams Family, another comedy that aired at the same time as *The Munsters*, also features a Frankenstein-like creature that is well known to classic TV buffs. Called Lurch, the monster on this show

The popular 1960s television series The Munsters *featured Herman Munster (right), a character who clearly resembled the 1931 movie version of Frankenstein's monster. The similarity ended there, with the TV character being both gentle and lovable.*

holds a job as a butler. Lurch is huge, gloomy, and slow-moving, and he speaks mostly in grunts and groans. However, he can talk when he wants to. "You rang?" he intones gloomily every time his employers summon him. Played by actor Ted Cassidy, Lurch has definitely lurched his way into the hearts of Frankenstein fans everywhere.

An Instantly Recognizable Figure

The Munsters and *The Addams Family* proved that Frankenstein's monster had a place on prime-time TV. In recent decades, the creature has found a home on two prominent late-night shows as well. His first notable appearance was on the sketch comedy show *Saturday Night Live* (*SNL*). Played in a recurring role by comedian Phil Hartman, *SNL*'s Frankenstein was a goofy version of Boris Karloff's classic creature. He grunted his signature phrase, "Fire BAD!" in response to every imaginable situation.

Less famous but equally funny is the monster that appeared regularly on the TV show *Late Night with Conan O'Brien* in the early 2000s. In a recurring sketch entitled "Frankenstein Wastes a Minute of Our Time," a speechless but manically cheerful monster does silly things that—no surprise here—waste about a minute of airtime. Pointless but hilarious, this creature was a favorite among *Conan* viewers.

Such creatures have been popular with other TV audiences as well. Over the years, characters inspired by Frankenstein's monster have popped up in countless hit series, including *Buffy the Vampire Slayer*, *The X-Files*, *Doctor Who*, and even children's shows such as *Wishbone*, *Sesame Street*, and *The Electric Company*. These characters usually have bit parts, often appearing in just one episode. But walk-on roles are just fine for a creature that needs no introduction. No matter what role he plays, Frankenstein's monster is instantly recognizable to TV viewers of all ages.

> # Did You Know?
>
> In 2002 LEGO produced and sold minifigures of Frankenstein and his infamous monster. The toys were part of the LEGO Studios line.

The Creature in Cartoons

This is true even when the creature is turned into a cartoon character. Usually modeled on the classic Universal Pictures look, animated versions of Frankenstein's monster have become a staple of the prime-time television lineup.

The title character of the 1960s series *Milton the Monster* had a particularly prominent role. Milton is a Frankenstein look-alike with a flat and seemingly hollow head. Vast quantities of steam erupt from Milton's head when the monster gets upset or excited. This does not happen too often, however, since Milton's scientist father used too much "tincture of tenderness" during the creation process. This accident turned Milton into a dopey, good-natured brute instead of the frightening sidekick his creator had intended.

The 1994 series *Monster Force* also gave Frankenstein's monster a starring role. This show pits six heroes known as the Monster Force against a group of evil beings dubbed the Creatures of the Night. Frankenstein, who also goes by simply "The Monster," is one of the good guys. He uses his immense strength and toughness to fight Dracula, the Creature from the Black Lagoon, and other wicked enemies of humanity.

> ## Did You Know?
>
> A pinball version of the 1994 film *Mary Shelley's Frankenstein* exists. The game was found in many arcades during the mid- to late 1990s.

Later animated shows did not showcase Frankenstein's monster to such a large degree. It seems that practically every popular cartoon series, however, has used him at least in passing. On one episode of *The Simpsons*, for example, a nerdy scientist named Professor Frink reanimates his dead father—who then horrifies his son by going on a hunt for a few replacement body parts. On *SpongeBob SquarePants*, SpongeBob doodles a Frankenstein-like picture that comes to life and terrorizes the town of Bikini Bottom. And the show *Ben 10: Alien Force* features an extraterrestrial antagonist that looks just like Frankenstein's creation.

Bernie Wrightson

In a 2008 interview, legendary horror illustrator Bernie Wrightson discusses his lifelong affinity for Frankenstein's monster. "Of all the archetypal monsters, Frankenstein was at the top of the list for me, followed by Wolfman, Creature from the Black Lagoon, Mummy . . . Dracula's pretty much at the bottom. I think it's just a personal preference. Frankenstein looks more interesting than Dracula. In terms of art, he's more fun to draw," the artist says.

Wrightson should know. He created more than 45 full-page images for *Bernie Wrightson's Frankenstein*, an illustrated version of Mary Shelley's novel that came out in 1994. A revised hardcover version containing even more artwork was published in 2008. Bringing Shelley's creation to twisted life, Wrightson's work is often cited as the best-ever rendition of Frankenstein's monster.

The artist's fascination with his subject matter undoubtedly gets part of the credit for this result. "[This work] was not an assignment, it was not a job. I would do the drawings in between paying gigs, when I had enough to be caught up with bills and groceries and what-not," Wrightson explains. "I would take three days here, a week there, to work on the *Frankenstein* volume. It took about seven years. . . . I've always had a thing for Frankenstein, and it was a labor of love."

Quoted in Edward Carey, "Spotlight on Bernie Wrightson," Comic Book Resources, June 16, 2008. www.comicbookresources.com.

These examples describe only a tiny fraction of Frankenstein's animated appearances and influences. During Halloween season, in particular, avoiding Frankenstein-related imagery and plotlines on TV is almost impossible. Without question, the vision that inspired Mary Shelley nearly 200 years ago is still inspiring today's television writers.

Author Inspiration

It is inspiring authors of a more literary bent as well. Many modern writers have reanimated Shelley's creation and used him as a character in their own novels. From horror and sci-fi to historical fiction and much more, Frankenstein's monster has appeared in written works of every imaginable genre.

Jean-Claude Carrière's *Frankenstein* series was among the earliest of these offerings. Published in 1957 and 1958, this six-book set begins in the frozen Arctic, where Shelley's original story leaves off. Instead of killing himself, the monster decides to return to Europe and terrorize the human population. Chapter after gory chapter of death and destruction are the horrifying result.

The Frankenstein Papers, another well-known adaptation of Shelley's work, was published in 1986. Written by science fiction author Fred Saberhagen, this novel claims to retell Shelley's story from the monster's point of view. It turns out that the monster has a very different perspective than Shelley did. His journal contains details about aliens, evil hunchbacks, and the American Revolution, among many other incredible things. It also describes the creature's budding friendship with American inventor Ben Franklin. Far-fetched and fantastic, this book is nonetheless popular among Frankenstein fans.

Dean Koontz's *Frankenstein* series, which started its publication run in 2004 and continues to the present day, has also found a following. Set in modern-day New Orleans, this collection tells the story of a still-living Victor Frankenstein. Frankenstein has aban-

> ## Did You Know?
>
> Frankenstein's monster was featured in a 1964 episode of *Bugs Bunny*. The robotic "Frankie" beats up the Tasmanian Devil and Bugs in classic cartoon fashion, leaving his victims bandaged and disheveled.

doned all of his human morals and is now single-mindedly determined to bring creatures to life. He will commit any act, no matter how heinous, that helps him to accomplish this goal. This work is utterly repellent to Frankenstein's original creation, who, like his master, is also still alive—although not, it must be said, entirely well. The hideously disfigured creature teams up with the New Orleans Police Department to stop the wretched Frankenstein from destroying the human race.

Koontz clearly remembers the moment that the inspiration for his *Frankenstein* series struck. "I thought, 'Ah, Frankenstein! And the monster is the good guy! That's good enough for me. I want to find out about this,'"[51] the author recalls in a 2010 radio interview. Already a prominent horror writer at the time, Koontz tackled his idea with ability and enthusiasm. The result is a series that builds upon the Frankenstein story in a modern, original, and sickeningly satisfying way.

Going Graphic

Yet some readers still want more. Not content with words alone, they want to actually watch the blood flying and the flesh decaying. They want to witness Frankenstein's awful laboratory with their own eyes. And most of all they want to shiver at the sight of Koontz's monster, who is described as being hideous beyond anything Shelley ever imagined.

Fans who feel this way have an easy way to satisfy their macabre cravings: They can pick up copies of *Prodigal Son Volume 1* and *Volume 2*. The result of a collaboration between Koontz and the writer/illustrator team of Chuck Dixon, Tim Seely, and Scott Cohn, these graphic novels present the first *Frankenstein* novel in a colorful, comiclike format. Checking in at 128 pages each, these books are not the typical newsstand fodder. They are serious reads that cater to people who appreciate horror art. Beautifully designed and executed, they have been well received by fans of Dean Koontz's series.

Prodigal Son may be the most recent entry in the graphic novel field, but it is far from the first Frankenstein-themed book to tread this ground. Frankenstein's monster has appeared in many other graphic novels and comics over the decades. Notable early examples include Dick Briefer's *Frankenstein* series, which ran in serial form from 1940 to 1954, and Marvel Comics' 1973 *The Monster of Frankenstein* cycle. The latter series was illustrated by Mike Ploog, who tried his utmost to make readers feel sympathy for his inhuman main character. "I related to that naïve monster wandering around a world he had no knowledge of—an outsider seeing everything through the eyes of a child,"[52] Ploog says in a 1998 interview.

The Ultimate Action Hero

Another often-mentioned graphic series is the 2004–2007 *Doc Frankenstein* collection. Illustrated by Steve Skroce and containing six volumes by early 2011, this series transports Frankenstein's monster into the modern world and turns him into an action-adventure hero. In doing so, it introduces profound changes to the creature's appearance and personality. One reviewer explains the new monster with these words:

> Gone is the green skin, replaced with an all-over blue hue. The hairdo is a crew cut instead of the literal flat-topped head, and the telltale neck electrodes have moved to his cranium. But the changes for this incarnation go far deeper. Certainly, he was born a grunting, brooding creature, but he has grown since his birth a couple hundred years ago. Now he is a brilliant, heroic figure, indestructible and effectively immortal.[53]

With his superhuman powers, Doc Frankenstein tries to help the human race. As always, however, he is horribly misunderstood. Revered by some people but feared by most, Skroce's monster struggles through yet another quest for love and acceptance.

Fun and Games

This struggle is usually minimized or eliminated altogether in video games, which have made good use of Shelley's creation over the

Selling Out

Over the decades, Frankenstein's monster has been the celebrity spokescreature for dozens of products. The creature has appeared in commercials for Twix candy bars, Shasta orange soda, Volkswagen vans, Radio Shack batteries, BIC pens, Reese's Peanut Butter Cups, and many other well-known items.

One particularly amusing ad features Teddy Ruxpin, an electronic talking bear that was a popular children's toy in the mid-1980s. The lifeless bear lies on Dr. Frankenstein's laboratory table, waiting to be imbued with the spark of life. When Frankenstein's scientific efforts fail, batteries come to the rescue. "It's alive!" Frankenstein cries as Teddy Ruxpin sits up and launches into a bedtime story.

The funniest Frankenstein-related ad of all might be for a product called Osteo Bi-Flex. In this 2004 commercial, the monster explains that all his stiffness and clumsiness disappeared when he started using an arthritis-relief cream. Clips of the happy, healthy creature doing yoga, giving banjo lessons, and gardening in a big straw hat play while the monster speaks. If Osteo Bi-Flex can cure this guy, the ad implies, it can certainly cure a regular human.

years. Frankenstein's monster has been a gaming staple since the earliest days of computer-generated play.

The first significant video-game offering was an Atari 2600 release called *Frankenstein's Monster*. Featuring simple, blocky graphics on a black screen, this game challenges players to build a brick wall around the monster before he can be reanimated. Poorly rendered ghosts, bats, spiders, and other obstacles interfere with this task. When the player fails—as he or she inevitably does—the monster comes to life. It stomps menacingly toward the computer screen until the viewing area is nothing but a green rectangle.

Another early game was Nintendo's *Frankenstein: The Monster Returns*. Released in 1991, this game features more sophisticated graphics and a more complex plotline than the Atari version. The game's premise involves a young woman named Emily who is kidnapped by Frankenstein's monster. The player must face the Grim Reaper and a host of other undead characters before finally reaching Frankenstein's lair. He or she must then overcome the monster to set Emily free.

Be the Monster

A few years later, a game called *Mary Shelley's Frankenstein* put a new twist on things. Rather than asking players to fight monsters, this Nintendo/Sega product lets them be the monster instead. Seeing everything from the viewpoint of the creature, players battle their way through several levels on a quest to exact revenge upon their creator, Victor Frankenstein. Along the way they must solve puzzles and use a stick to fight off angry peasants. Released in 1994 to tie in with the film of the same name, this game truly lets players walk in the creature's frightful footsteps.

The same is true in a 1996 game called *Frankenstein: Through the Eyes of the Monster*. This product uses interactive movies to put players into the creature's clunky shoes. The game begins when the player is resurrected by Frankenstein, who is played with creepy intensity by actor Tim Curry (who, incidentally, also portrayed Frank-N-Furter in *The Rocky Horror Picture Show*). Players explore the scientist's laboratory and castle to discover the truth about their death and reanimation—and, hopefully, to return themselves to human form.

These games used Frankenstein's monster as a main character. But this is not the case in all games. Shelley's creation has snagged many bit parts in the gaming world. He pops up briefly in titles as diverse as *Castlevania*, *Darkstalkers*, *Warriors of Primetime*, *MadWorld*, and even *Donkey Kong* and *RollerCoaster Tycoon*. Whatever role he plays, the monster adds some classic flair to a totally modern format.

Terrible Tunes

Popular music is another format that was unheard of in Shelley's time. Today, though, music is an integral part of people's daily lives—and it has become yet another vehicle for Frankenstein's monster. Through concepts, lyrics, and even music videos, the creature is helping modern Frankenstein fans to sing a whole new tune.

The most popular of these tunes is undoubtedly the 1962 novelty hit "Monster Mash." Written and performed by Bobby Pickett, this song is narrated by a Frankenstein-like mad scientist. It tells the musical tale of the doctor's creation, who comes to life one night and invents a dance that becomes "a graveyard smash."[54] Reaching #1 on the *Billboard* Hot 100 chart soon after its release, "Monster Mash" has now been re-recorded dozens of times by other artists and is considered a Halloween classic.

Also a classic is Sam Cooke's 1963 song entitled "Another Saturday Night." While this song has nothing to do with Shelley's story, it does contain a now-famous reference to the tale's monster. "Another fella told me he had a sister who looked just fine. Instead of being my deliverance, she had a strange resemblance to a cat named Frankenstein,"[55] Cooke sings in his classic hit.

Bearing even less apparent relationship to Shelley's story is "Frankenstein," a 1973 instrumental that is immediately recognizable to any classic-rock enthusiast. Performed by the Edgar Winter Group, this song got its name from its stitched-together origins. Edgar Winter remembers that the band's members were sitting in a music studio one day among bits of recorded tape, trying to assemble a usable piece of music. "Wow, man, it's like Frankenstein," drummer Chuck Ruff muttered at one point—and the title stuck. "When you hear [the song's] theme, you can just see that hulking monster, that hulking, lumbering monster. I couldn't have written something

> **Did You Know?**
>
> The band Phish regularly plays the Edgar Winter Group's "Frankenstein" during live performances.

that sounded more like Frankenstein if I'd been thinking about it,"[56] Winter said in a 2010 interview.

Speaking the Lingo

Winter's story is a good example of a trend that has occurred in the popular view of Frankenstein's monster. Today, people tend to associate anything that seems to be hastily or carelessly assembled with Shelley's creature. The English language now includes many examples of this tendency.

One of these examples has been gracing rock concert arenas since the late 1970s. Eddie Van Halen, the lead guitarist of the group Van Halen, plays an instrument he affectionately refers to as the "Frankenstrat." The guitar is a cobbled-together assemblage of parts from various manufacturers. Van Halen constantly tinkers with his creation, adding new components and art elements to create fresh looks and sounds.

The same kind of tinkering occurs on a larger scale in the automotive world. Custom car and motorcycle enthusiasts often build vehicles from the ground up, using whatever parts they can find or buy. The results of these efforts are referred to as "Frankensteins" or, in the motorcycling world, as "Frankenbikes." Containing a little bit of this and a little bit of that, these creations are the mechanical cousins of Frankenstein's monster.

The beast has relatives in the grocery business, too. In the modern world, certain foods are routinely created by genetic manipulation or

Possibly the most enduring image of Mary Shelley's monster can be seen in Boris Karloff's character from the 1931 movie Frankenstein *(pictured). The corpselike skin, black hair, scars, and prominent electrical bolts have formed an indelible image in the public mind.*

other scientific tricks. Many people distrust these foods, considering them unnatural and possibly even dangerous. The term "Frankenfood," which was coined in the early 1990s, embodies this attitude. "[It] sums up nicely the monstrous unnaturalness of such controversial new products as genetically enhanced tomatoes and chromosome-tinkered cows,"[57] one reporter wrote soon after the term emerged. Evoking images of an irresponsible Frankenstein in his awful laboratory, the word "Frankenfood" melds an everyday item with an implied judgment in one handy term.

The term has become popular not just because it is evocative. The prefix "Franken-," it turns out, is universally useful as well. People have discovered that it works for just about any item, not just "food" as a general category. As a result, critics today routinely "Franken-"ize anything they consider scientifically creepy. Examples include "Frankencow," "Frankencorn," "Frankenfish," "Frankenveggies," and countless others. The farmers who produce these items, amusingly but not surprisingly, are sometimes dubbed "Frankenfarmers."

> ## Did You Know?
>
> The term "Frankenfood," which refers to genetically modified foods, first appeared in the *New York Times* in a June 2, 1992, letter to the editor. The word was invented by Paul Lewis, a professor of English at Boston College.

This usage seems to be more than just a trend. In a move that signals increasing acceptance, definitions of the prefix "Franken-" now appear in many minor dictionaries. Chances are good that the term will soon show up in major dictionaries as well. If it does, this particular pop culture creation will be a fixture of the English language for a long, long time to come.

Ghoulish Grab Bag

Other usages of Shelley's monster will probably prove just as tenacious. For instance, a Halloween without Frankenstein imagery is hard to imagine. Stores today sell everything from Frankenstein costumes to candy, toys, stuffed dolls, clothing, and anything else a Frankenstein fan could possibly desire. Most of these creations follow Boris Karloff's lead, portraying a monster with green skin, black hair, scars, and prominent electrical bolts. This instantly recognizable image acts as a sort of cultural shortcut to holiday chills and thrills.

When it comes to costumes, the Bride of Frankenstein has become a Halloween fixture as well. A black-and-white wig, a flowing white gown, and ghoulish makeup complete the look of this creature. Classic yet creepy, the Bride is a popular choice for trick-or-treaters and partygoers of all ages.

Without doubt, the Bride and her horrible husband-to-be get extra exposure around Halloween. But these creatures, particularly Frankenstein's original male creature, have managed to permeate popular culture in every season. In grocery stores, for example, Frankenstein's monster has been the face of General Mills's Franken Berry cereal since the early 1970s. Pink instead of the typical green, this cartoon creation hawks a sugary corn-and-marshmallow concoction. This fiendishly friendly treat has been a breakfast staple for generations of children.

Nowadays, Frankenstein-themed greeting cards are a staple as well. Shelley's creature spouts birthday wishes, apologies, party invitations, words of love, and even baby announcements. Offering pun-heavy plays on "alive," "stitches," "monstrous," "shocking," and other words that evoke Shelley's story, these cards make Frankenstein's monster relevant for practically every occasion.

And the examples do not end there. Frankenstein's monster, it seems, is everywhere. The fiend can be found today on postage stamps, in children's coloring books, and on the radio. He shows up in corporate newsletters, on restaurant menus, and on cosmetics packaging. He lends his name to a lime-green line of Nike sneakers and a catnip scratch toy. He has even been reanimated as a rubber duckie—squeaker included.

Shelley's Vision Endures

This final example shows just how ubiquitous history's favorite monster has become. Green-feathered, staple-studded, and wearing a shredded tuxedo jacket, the Frankenstein duckie bears no actual resemblance to the literary creation on which it is based. Yet nearly 200 years after *Frankenstein* hit bookshelves, the duck is immediately identifiable to people everywhere. This fact is a testament to the enduring power of Shelley's vision. Terrifying in 1816 and equally terrifying today, this author's nightmare will probably be haunting humankind for centuries to come.

Source Notes

Chapter One: A Nightmare Comes True

1. Quoted in Emily W. Sunstein, *Mary Shelley: Romance and Reality*. Baltimore: Johns Hopkins University Press, 1991, p. 58.
2. Mary Shelley, author's introduction to *Frankenstein*, introduction and notes by Karen Karbiener. New York: Barnes & Noble Classics, 2003, pp. 8–9.
3. Shelley, author's introduction to *Frankenstein*, p. 9.
4. Mary Shelley, *Frankenstein*, chap. 2, Literature.org: The Online Literature Library. www.literature.org.
5. Shelley, *Frankenstein*, chap. 4.
6. Shelley, *Frankenstein*, chap. 10.
7. Shelley, *Frankenstein*, chap. 20.
8. Shelley, *Frankenstein*, chap. 23.
9. John Wilson Croker, "Review of *Frankenstein*," *Quarterly Review*, vol. 18, no. 36, January 1818, pp. 379–85. www.crossref-it.info.
10. *Literary Panorama and National Register*, "Review of *Frankenstein*," June 1, 1818, pp. 411–14. www.rc.umd.edu.
11. Walter Scott, "Review of *Frankenstein*," *Blackwood's Edinburgh Magazine 2*, March 20/April 1, 1818, pp. 613–20. www.rc.umd.edu.
12. Croker, "Review of *Frankenstein*."
13. Denise Evans and Mary L. Onorato, eds., "*Frankenstein; or, The Modern Prometheus*; Mary Wollstonecraft Shelley—Introduction," *Nineteenth-Century Literary Criticism*, vol. 59. Farmington Hills, MI: Gale Cengage, 1997. www.enotes.com.

Chapter Two: Anatomy of a Monster

14. Matthew Gunia, "A Story Greatly Superior to Stereotyped Frankenstein," Amazon.com reviews, June 30, 2001. www.amazon.com.
15. Andreas Rohrmoser, "Introduction," Frankenstein Films. www.frankensteinfilms.com.

16. Shelley, *Frankenstein*, chap. 4.

17. Shelley, *Frankenstein*, chap. 5.

18. Shelley, *Frankenstein*, chap. 4.

19. Shelley, *Frankenstein*, chap. 4.

20. Shelley, *Frankenstein*, chap. 5.

21. Shelley, *Frankenstein*, chap. 24.

22. Shelley, *Frankenstein*, chap. 10.

23. Shelley, *Frankenstein*, chap. 14.

24. Gunia, "A Story Greatly Superior to Stereotyped Frankenstein."

25. Shelley, *Frankenstein*, chap. 11.

26. Shelley, *Frankenstein*, chap. 11.

27. Shelley, *Frankenstein*, chap 13.

28. Harold Bloom, introduction to *Mary Shelley's "Frankenstein."* New York: Chelsea House, 1996, p. 6. www.scribd.com.

29. Shelley, *Frankenstein*, chap. 15.

30. Shelley, *Frankenstein*, chap. 12.

31. Shelley, *Frankenstein*, chap. 16.

32. Shelley, *Frankenstein*, chap. 16.

33. Shelley, *Frankenstein*, chap. 16.

34. Shelley, *Frankenstein*, chap. 17.

35. Ian Fowler, "A Moving, Disturbing, Depressing, but Also Touching Tale," review, Amazon.com, December 31, 2004. www.amazon.com.

36. Shelley, *Frankenstein*, chap. 24.

37. Shelley, *Frankenstein*, chap. 24.

Chapter Three: Retelling the Tale on Stage and Screen

38. Quoted in Chris Baldick, *In Frankenstein's Shadow: Myth, Monstrosity, and Nineteenth-Century Writing*. Oxford: Oxford University Press, 1990, p. 58.

39. Henry M. Milner, *Frankenstein; or, The Man and the Monster: A Melodrama in Two Acts*. London: J. Duncombe, 1826, 1.iii.

40. Karen Karbiener, "Inspired by Frankenstein," in Mary Shelley, *Frankenstein*, introduction and notes by Karen Karbiener, p. 213.

41. Andreas Rohrmoser, "A Face for the Monster: The Universal Pictures Series, *Frankenstein* (1931)," Frankenstein Films. www.frankensteinfilms.com.

42. *Frankenstein*, directed by James Whale, Universal Pictures, 1931.

43. *Bride of Frankenstein*, directed by James Whale, Universal Pictures, 1935.

44. Andreas Rohrmoser, "A Face for the Monster: The Universal Pictures Series, *Bride of Frankenstein* (1935)," Frankenstein Films. www.frankensteinfilms.com.

45. Helen Wheatley, "*Mystery and Imagination:* Anatomy of a Gothic Anthology Series," in *Small Screen, Big Ideas: Television in the 1950s*, ed. Janet Thumim. London: I.B. Taurus & Co., 2002, p. 166.

46. Michael F. Housel, "Dan Curtis' *Frankenstein*," review, Amazon.com, December 7, 2007. www.amazon.com.

47. Bradley Beard, "The BEST Novel to Screen Adaptation Yet!!" review, Amazon.com, October 6, 2004. www.amazon.com.

48. Derek Armstrong, "Review of *The Rocky Horror Picture Show*," All Movie. www.allmovie.com.

49. Kenneth Branagh, *Mary Shelley's Frankenstein: A Classic Tale of Terror Reborn on Film*. New York: Newmarket Press, 1994, p. 20.

Chapter Four: Frankenstein in Popular Culture

50. Shelley, *Frankenstein*, chap. 24.

51. Dean Koontz, interview by Matthew Peterson, "Dragons and Creatures," The Author Hour, VoiceAmerica, January 21, 2010.

52. Mike Ploog, interview by Jon B. Cooke, "The Man Called Ploog," Comic Book Artist #2, TwoMorrows, May 31, 1988. www.twomorrows.com.

53. Louis Vitella, "Review: Doc Frankenstein #1," ComicCritique.com, January 2005. www.comiccritique.com..

54. Bobby Pickett and the Crypt-Kickers, "Monster Mash," *The Original Monster Mash*, Garpax Records, 1962.

55. Sam Cooke, "Another Saturday Night," *Ain't That Good News*, RCA, 1963.

56. Quoted in Steve Marinucci, "Edgar Winter Says He's Ready to Rock 'n Rol-l-l-l Again with Ringo Starr – Part 2: 'Frankenstein,'" *Examiner National*, April 16, 2010. www.examiner.com.

57. Mark Muro, "He Created a Monster Word," *Boston Globe*, October 14, 1992, p. 75.

For Further Exploration

Nonfiction Books

Harold Bloom, *Bloom's Modern Critical Views: Percy Shelley*. New York: Chelsea House, 2009. This book examines the works and biography of Percy Bysshe Shelley, Mary Shelley's husband.

Catherine Wells, *Strange Creatures: The Story of Mary Shelley*. Greensboro, NC: Morgan Reynolds, 2009. Written for teens, this book offers a lively biography of *Frankenstein*'s author.

Gary Wiener, *Bioethics in Mary Shelley's "Frankenstein."* Farmington Hills, MI: Greenhaven, 2010. Part of the Social Issues in Literature series, this book examines some of the ethical questions raised by Mary Shelley's historic novel.

Fiction Books

Michael Burgan and Dennis Calero, *Mary Shelley's "Frankenstein."* Mankato, MN: Stone Arch Books, 2007. This graphic novel is a colorful yet faithful retelling of Shelley's story.

Lisi Harrison, *Monster High*. New York: Little, Brown, 2010. Read about the high-school misadventures of Frankie Stein, a recently reanimated teenage monster.

Susan Heyboer O'Keefe, *Frankenstein's Monster*. New York: Three Rivers, 2010. This novel is a sequel to Mary Shelley's *Frankenstein*. In tone, setting, and details, it is true to the original in every way possible.

Kenneth Oppel, *This Dark Endeavor: The Apprenticeship of Victor Frankenstein*. New York: Simon & Schuster, 2011. This fictional work from a favorite author of young adult books puts a new twist on Victor Frankenstein's life and adventures.

Mary Shelley, *Frankenstein*. Oxford: Oxford University Press, 2010. Shelley's novel is one of the best horror books of all time. It is a must-read for any Frankenstein fan.

Bram Stoker, *The New Annotated "Dracula."* Edited by Leslie S. Klinger. New York: Norton, 2008. With its roots in the same contest that created *Frankenstein*, this horror classic is well worth reading.

Websites

Fan Fiction (www.fanfiction.net). This site includes a sizeable collection of Frankenstein-related fiction created by modern fans of Mary Shelley's monster.

Frankenstein Films (www.frankensteinfilms.com). This excellent site offers commentary and reviews on dozens of Frankenstein-related films and products, along with a good overview of Shelley's original novel.

Monster Librarian (www.monsterlibrarian.com). This site offers reviews and information on horror books of all types, along with many good articles and author interviews.

Monstrous (www.monstrous.com). Extensive information on every imaginable monster, including Frankenstein, can be found on this site.

Project Gutenberg (www.gutenberg.org). This website offers free, full-text versions of over 100,000 classic works, including Mary Shelley's *Frankenstein*.

YouTube (www.youtube.com). The 1910 silent-film version of *Frankenstein*, along with countless other Frankenstein-related productions, can be viewed at no charge on this site.

Index

Picture Credits

About the Author

Kris Hirschmann has written more than 200 books for children. She owns and runs a business that provides a variety of writing and editorial services. She lives just outside Orlando, Florida, with her husband, Michael, and her daughters Nikki and Erika.